SEEKING THE SOVEREIGN

A SPECULATIVE FICTION NOVELLA

THE NEXT HIGH PRIEST
BOOK 1

PETER DEHAAN

Credits:

- Creative Consultants: Lisa Baker and Joanna K. Harris
- Developmental editor: Julie Harbison
- Copyeditor: Robyn Mulder
- Cover design: Fanderclai Design
- Author photo: Chelsie Jensen Photography

To all who seek more from life.

CONTENTS

SEEKING THE SOVEREIGN

In a world just like ours . . . only different

The Sovereign will replace the fallen one with another from an unknown tribe who will restore what once was and usher in a new era. The people will marvel and be amazed. - Prophecy 11.41

1

FORBIDDEN

Emma strode with confidence down the hall toward fifth-period Advanced Algebra, her hazel hair flouncing on her back with each step. As usual, Chloe walked on her right. A more recent development was Joshua trailing behind. His presence, lanky and loitering, annoyed Emma. He was like a third wheel on a bicycle. His constant hovering threatened to come between her and Chloe. But she had said nothing—so far—because he was Chloe's friend.

A commotion arose. A cocky jock had backed a new girl into the lockers. He pointed a threatening finger at the poor girl's face. She trembled.

Without thinking, Emma shoved her algebra book at Chloe and rushed forward like a charging bull. She reached up to grab the muscle-bound jerk's bicep and spun him around. "Stop harassing her."

"You telling me what to do?" Narrowing his gaze, he glared down at Emma.

"The Sovereign demands justice. The unjust will perish along with their folly."

"Are you quoting the Holy Text to me?" The guy shook his head. "Freak."

He backed away from Emma and gave the terrified new girl one last shove. Her back slammed against the lockers, she dropped her books, and her body slumped to the floor.

Emma bent down. "You okay?"

The girl looked up at Emma, eyelids fluttering. She opened her mouth, but no words came out.

"He's gone." Emma picked up the girl's things and extended her hand. "Can you get up?"

"Think so." The girl's words came out soft and shaky. "Thanks for saving me." With care, she rose and scurried away.

Emma returned to an open-mouthed Chloe. "That was intense." The pint-sized girl shuddered, the tips of her black hair bouncing on her shoulders. "I've never seen you like that."

"I wasn't thinking," Emma said. "It's like I was

on autopilot or something and couldn't stop myself."

"That was very brave. And a bit crazy." Chloe stared at Emma's shaking body. "Now let me ask, are *you* okay?"

Emma nodded and tried to take a step forward, but she wobbled. Her body quivered, her head tipped to the side, and everything went black. As she fell, she sensed a pair of strong arms catching her.

The next thing she knew, she was leaning against some lockers, her head spinning. Chloe steadied her on one side and Joshua was on the other. His gentle touch comforted her, filling her with warmth. He'd never been so close to her.

Emma looked up into his eyes, noticing them for the first time. *How could I have missed this brilliant brown?* His eyes sparkled as the most beautiful things Emma had ever seen. For Chloe's sake, she pushed these thoughts out of her mind.

"Thanks." Emma slowly drew in a deep breath. "I'll be okay."

"Are you sure?" Concern covered Chloe's face.

Emma nodded.

"Really sure?" Joshua double-checked.

"For sure." Emma nodded to confirm. *But am I?*

"Okay. Got to go. Can't be late for class." Joshua spun around and dashed in the opposite direction. Chloe guided Emma to algebra.

"I'm so glad your friend was there to catch me," Emma said.

"My friend? I thought he was *your* friend. That's why I never said anything about him following you around like a little lost puppy."

"Whatever." Emma didn't want to think any more about Joshua. She tried to shove the image of his beautiful brown eyes out of her mind.

Her last two classes flashed by in a blur. Before Emma knew it, the school day ended. She and Chloe waited outside the main doors for the rest of their group to join them. Though so far there had never been an incident while walking home alone, the increase in patrols scooping up people made traveling as a posse a wise move. And the sudden disappearance of Mrs. Butler, their religion teacher, added to their concern.

As Emma's classmates walked up, many cele-brated what she had done.

"You go, girl," Isabella said.

Lane offered a fist bump.

"About time someone put him in his place," Lauren added.

Emma received their affirmations, but her mind was far away. She slipped her hand into the pocket of her jeans and touched her babysitting money. Today she would make a different choice. Today she would embrace the opportunity the Sovereign set before her. She tried to recall the words of the Holy Text she'd read the night before. "The Sovereign blesses you to bless others." This was something to contemplate.

"Emma," Chloe murmured out of the corner of her mouth. "Earth to Emma, come in Emma."

A startled Emma snapped her attention back to the present. The last of the group had arrived. All twelve friends were ready, waiting for her to lead them home. "Okay, let's go. The question for today is, 'What are you thankful for?'"

She turned and headed out, leading their disparate band home. Chloe walked next to her while Joshua trailed behind. If Joshua wasn't Chloe's friend—and he wasn't hers—why was he always hanging around? Did he like Chloe? *Does he like me?* Emma shuddered. She shook off the thought. She didn't have time to be distracted by a boyfriend.

The group was quiet. Emma hoped it was because they were thinking about her question. At last Lane spoke. "I'm thankful I passed my algebra test today."

"And I'm thankful for no chemistry homework," Isabella said. Everyone chuckled.

Others soon shared their thankfulness. Some ideas were trivial and others were thoughtful, but everyone was sincere.

They stopped at a crosswalk, waiting for the light to change. In the next block perched a homeless man—*the* homeless man—right where they were headed. With tangled, white hair and a scruffy beard, the man sat cross-legged on the sidewalk. A cardboard carton lay next to him. It was illegal for people to ask for money or hold up a sign, but setting out a donation box was a loophole in the law. Every homeless person knew this.

Until today, Emma had rerouted their group so they wouldn't cross paths with the strange man. Even for a homeless person, he was extra odd. The soiled and tattered robe he always wore most likely used to be white. Though he was never in the same place, he was somewhere on their path every day. Today she would not avoid him.

"Should we turn?" Chloe tipped her head to the right. "That homeless guy creeps me out."

"He's quite harmless," Joshua declared.

"The Holy Text says, 'Give to all who ask and are in need' and 'the Sovereign loves . . .'" Emma paused, trying to recall the rest of the passage she'd read the night before.

"The Sovereign loves a generous heart," Joshua said as he moved to walk on Emma's other side.

She cast a curious look at this perplexing boy. With wide-eyed astonishment and in a near whisper, she asked, "You know the Holy Text?"

"I read it every morning."

Chloe gasped. Her eyebrows arched. "Ordinary people can't read the Holy Text. It's forbidden."

"Says who?" The words spewed from Emma's mouth more forcibly than she intended, harsher than she wanted. But she didn't know if she could have held them back anyway.

Chloe's gaze darted to Emma. "Well . . . like everyone." She scrutinized Emma as if she were crazy and then cast an incredulous look toward Joshua. "You two could get in trouble. Lots of it." Then the worried girl lowered her voice. "You could even get arrested and sent for retraining."

"I must do what I must do." Emma wasn't usually one to speak without thinking, but lately her mouth was one step ahead of her mind. It all started when she began studying the Holy Text in secret.

The crosswalk light turned green. "Today we go straight," Emma said.

With a confident stride on the outside and her heart thumping on the inside, Emma reached into her pocket and pulled out the money she'd set aside for this moment. Flashing her best smile, she approached the man to drop the cash into his box. As she bent toward him, his body odor assaulted her unsuspecting nostrils. She almost gagged, but she hoped he didn't notice or take offense.

"Bless you, my child," he said. "May the Sovereign protect you and keep your disciples safe in the days ahead." His weathered face shone with the kindness that she could only see from up close, but his stench nauseated her.

Disciples? Clearly, this man isn't playing with a full deck.

"I speak of what is true." He dipped his head down as if to confirm his words.

Did he just read my mind? Emma pushed that idea away, just in case she might be right. As she continued past him, she willed her mind to go blank —to think of nothing—as if that were possible.

Behind her, the group shuffled by him to catch

up with her, murmuring concern over the man's situation. But she didn't think anyone else gave him any money. *Maybe tomorrow they'll act differently.*

Their company continued east. As they did, smaller groups would peel off and head toward their respective homes. Before long, their number was down to four. Emma and Chloe went one way while Joshua and Lane headed in the opposite direction.

"You were amazing today at school," Chloe said when they got to her house.

"I was stupid," Emma answered. "Won't make that mistake again."

After waving goodbye, Emma cut through back-yards to avoid any patrols and work her way home.

2

DINNER AND DISHES

Emma's family of five held hands around the dinner table as her dad asked for the Sovereign's blessing on the meal. Tuesday was pasta night, and her mom had prepared Emma's favorite—spaghetti and meatballs, toasted garlic bread, green beans, and, for dessert, tiramisu. Since she was almost sixteen, Emma's parents now allowed her small sips of diluted wine on pasta night, a decision that vexed the twins to no end.

The family shared their joys and struggles of the day. Emma's sister, Hailey, and brother, Brayden, reveled in the version of her exploits that had trickled over to the middle school. Though based on truth, their version of Emma's courage lifted her to near sainthood.

Seeking to defuse the attention, Emma glanced at her dad. "May I say our concluding prayer tonight?"

"Certainly."

"Sovereign Lord, we thank you for your . . . provisions for the day." Emma struggled to make her words sound grown-up and mature. "For protection . . . and guidance. For your grace and mercy." The words tumbled out. "May we end our day with a grateful heart for who you are and what you have done. Amen."

"I'm sure your words pleased the Sovereign," her dad said.

"Whose turn is it to help with dishes?" Emma's mom asked this every night, even though everyone always knew the schedule.

"Not us!" Hailey and Brayden exclaimed in unison, as if displaying their special twin connection. "May we be excused?" they asked in tandem.

"Certainly," their dad said with a nod. "But homework first before anything else." He said this every night.

The twins scampered off. Emma's parents stood and picked up their plates. Emma remained seated. She had something on her mind. "What would you think if we added something to the end of our evening meal? A new practice?"

Emma's parents paused from clearing the table and looked at her. Her dad spoke first. "What do you have in mind?"

Emma's heart pounded. "What if after the meal and before the concluding prayer we read from a portion of the Holy Text?" She shifted her glance from her dad to her mom and back to her dad, searching for a clue about what either was thinking.

"Emma!" Her mom's eyes opened wide in disbelief. "Normal people don't read Scripture. It's only for priests."

"But who says? And why? We have a copy on the shelf in our living room. It's on display like a shrine. Why not read it instead of just looking at it?"

"Emma, everyone owns a copy of the Holy Text." Her dad's gentle tone exuded patience. His eyes radiated love toward his oldest daughter. "It's what everyone does. What we're supposed to do."

"But why?" Emma asked again. "Mrs. Butler said that two hundred years ago most everyone read the Holy Text."

"Perhaps that's why they arrested her," Mom said.

Emma pushed that thought aside. "It's as if we worship the Holy Text instead of the Sovereign. Aren't you the least bit curious about what it says?"

"We have the High Priest to teach us what we need to know . . . at least we did." Emma's mom paused as she considered what to say next. "And now we have His Royal Eminence to guide us in spiritual matters."

The three of them cleared the rest of the table in silence. Emma's dad left to make sure the twins were doing their homework, which they all knew was highly unlikely. Emma and her mom worked on the dishes, handling their task with rote precision.

At last Emma spoke. "I get that we're expected to have a copy of the Holy Text, but what I don't get is why we don't read it."

Her mom opened her mouth to speak but said nothing.

Emma finished drying a plate and set it down a little too hard. "Can't the Sovereign reveal truth to us? To any of us, whether or not we're a priest?"

"Emma, this must stop! It borders on heresy." Her mom's words were firm. "Your father and I trained you to be an independent thinker, but this is too much. Spouting such unorthodox ideas could get you in trouble. Arrests of heretics have been on the increase ever since the High Priest died."

"I'm sorry, Mother." Calling her *Mother* instead of *Mom* was Emma's small way of showing her displeasure. She didn't know if her mom caught the distinction, but it provided a small sense of satisfaction.

"We encouraged you to pursue your dreams, but maybe we went too far when we said you could accomplish anything or do anything."

"I'm glad for how you raised me and what you taught me." Emma dried the last plate and placed it on top of the others in the cabinet. "I still want to be an architect when I grow up, but I wonder if there's more. I want more."

"You mean like to start your own firm or teach at university?"

Emma shook her head. "I mean more spiritually."

Emma's mom dried her hands and turned to face her. "Isn't a career in architecture and a family of your own enough?"

"Yes . . . but," Emma sputtered, "I also want to read the Holy Text and to hear the Sovereign speak to me like the prophets of old. Is that too much to ask? Too much to hope for?"

"Though it's unfair, all priests are male." Her dad's voice wafted in from behind. "Only priests have the needed training to read and understand Scripture. That's the way it is. No matter how badly you want it to happen, that's not something you can change."

"Your father's right, dear." Her mom reached up and brushed a stray strand of hazel hair from Emma's cheek, tucking it behind her ear.

"Though some of the ancients heard from the Sovereign, that era has passed," her dad said. "For whatever reason, we're now living in an era of silence. The Sovereign remains distant and aloof. That leaves the High Priest—when we have one—and His Royal Eminence to teach us. We need to accept this as fact and be content with what we have."

Emma didn't trust herself to speak without getting emotional, so she just nodded.

Her mom gave her a sideways hug, and her dad landed a quick kiss on her forehead. "We love you . . . more than anything," he said.

Emma swallowed hard and forced a smile. "Now, to tackle my homework. I have a ton." A surge of guilt overcame her for lying to her parents . . . again. But they wouldn't understand. Of that, she was sure—now more than ever.

Her dad nodded his assent, but her mom voiced concern. "You're always doing homework. Are they giving you too much? Perhaps I should have a chat with Principal Johnson."

"No need, Mom . . . this is, ah . . . more like extra credit. It's all good."

"Just don't push yourself too hard."

Emma retreated to her bedroom.

3

HOMEWORK

Over the past several months, an urgency had stirred in Emma's soul, a call to propel her spirit to a higher plane. It drove her on a quest for a much grander reality, one that transcended her physical existence.

Am I crazy? Perhaps. Can I stop? No way.

An unseen unction compelled her to reach out and grasp what she could not see, what no one at home or the Temple services had ever mentioned. Without someone to guide her, she had dived into the Holy Text in search of truth.

It was obvious her parents didn't understand. Although they practiced their faith rituals without fault, they had never read the Scriptures. No one did. The only attention their copy of the Holy Text ever received was an occasional dusting.

Emma pursued a different path. She studied her copy of the Text in secret. As she did, her classes took on new meaning. She saw the Sovereign's hand in everything she learned.

In math, with the organized, absolute perfection of numbers. Factors, squares, and primes. The delightful infinity of pi and the precision of finding one answer to every problem. Math was her favorite class, no doubt fueled by the affinity for numbers she had inherited from her mom.

Next came biology, with the Sovereign's fingerprints on every living creature. As a physician, her dad's domain was science, which she embraced as well. And the Fibonacci sequence connected math with science in a mind-blowing way.

History also reflected the Almighty's hand at work. And art allowed Emma to create in celebration of her Creator. For anyone willing to look, each class pointed to the Sovereign.

It took her mere minutes to complete her algebra, Honors Bio, and English homework. All of it.

Now, on to what mattered most, what excited her more than anything.

She tiptoed to her door and peeked down the

hall to make sure no one was there. Her parents would never understand what she was about to do, what she did every night.

Retreating inside, she slid the door shut and clicked the lock. Alone at last. She let out a slow sigh. Her mom had said that normal people couldn't approach the Sovereign, much less receive divine insight. But Emma now wondered if her mom might be wrong. After all, what does an accountant know about religion?

Emma retrieved her copy of the Holy Text from its prominent place on her bookshelf. When she had bought the book with her babysitting money, the idea shocked her mom. "Well, you'll need a copy when you get married and have your own home. So I guess it's okay to get it early. Let me buy you a stand, so you can display it properly." It had been easier for Emma to agree than explain she intended to read the book, not exhibit it.

With care, Emma laid the sacred book on the floor. Going to her bed, she slipped her hand between the mattress and box spring to pull out her well-worn journal. She set it next to the Holy Text. She lit two candles, which she stationed on each side of the books, and turned off the lights.

Though she wanted to begin right away, she

had a ritual to complete first. Though not a prescribed rite, it was something she'd developed over time, fine-tuning it as she went.

It was a physical act of worship that prepared her heart and her mind to bathe in the words of Scripture. Yet it also possessed an almost superstitious obligation that she must complete—fully and without variation—if she hoped to receive the supernatural insight that she sought from the sacred text. In her soul, she knew this to be in error, but she dared not abandon this practice. Why? Because it produced results. Every time.

Emma kneeled before the Holy Text and lowered her head toward it until her forehead touched its regal, leather cover. Its coolness bathed her brow and sent peace surging through her body. After three seconds, she straightened her torso and raised her arms heavenward. "Guide my reading, oh Sovereign Spirit."

She bowed a second time and straightened to say, "Guide my study, oh Sovereign Lord."

She bowed a third time and again lifted her arms toward the Almighty's abode. "Guide my meditation, oh Sovereign Master."

Yes, it was a silly ritual, but it prepared her heart and mind to learn and understand.

Now ready to begin, she opened to the pages marked by the book's maroon ribbon. She read. She studied. And she meditated. She scribbled notes furiously in her journal. She stayed hunched in this kneeling position, as if to mortify her body and open her spirit. Uncomfortable? Yes. Beneficial? Even more.

It seemed she'd just begun when the gentle tapping of a knuckle on her door roused her. "Ten o'clock, Emma," her dad said. "Time to wrap up."

Her soul groaned. "Yes, Father." *How had two hours passed so fast?*

Emma returned the Scripture to its ostentatious stand, slid her journal back into its hiding place, and blew out both candles. Without turning on a light, she changed into her nightgown and snuggled into bed under her fluffy down comforter. Within seconds she was asleep.

That night, a vision pushed into her slumber. She'd had short visions a few times in the past. At first, they alarmed her. They seemed more real than dreams. These experiences made no sense, but they supernaturally satiated her whenever they occurred.

This vision placed her in someone's backyard. Though the neighborhood seemed familiar, she didn't recognize the house. The backyard had several gigantic oaks, just like the yards on either side. But the grandest tree of all supported an elevated playhouse.

Climb, a voice said. It came from within her mind, yet it originated from without. It was not a command to trifle with. In her spirit, Emma ran to the ladder and scampered up it to reach the elevated structure. *Sanctuary*, the voice said. *A safe place.*

Emma awoke with a start. Her face burned and sweat drenched her nightgown. In the dark, she stumbled to her dresser, pulled out a T-shirt, and changed. *Much better.* She climbed back into bed, feeling perplexed by her strange vision.

Was this a message from the Sovereign? What does it mean?

4

PRIORITIES

Exhausted from her ordeal during the night, Emma got up and readied herself for school. Mechanically, she showered, dressed, and ate breakfast. Preoccupied, she trudged off to Chloe's house. She knocked on the front door and was still in a daze when a bright-eyed Chloe bounded out. "Morning, girlfriend!"

The greeting snapped Emma back to reality— sort of. "Morning."

The pair headed off without saying another word. At last, Chloe broke the silence. "You're awfully quiet this morning. Something wrong?"

"I kind of got in a fight with Mom last night." Emma scrunched her eyebrows and shook off the thought. "It was more like a disagreement. She doesn't get me—and won't even try. Then I had the strangest of dreams. The thing with Mom must have triggered it."

"Just be glad your mom is part of your life."

Her friend's response turned Emma's inward focus to Chloe's situation. "I'm sorry."

"Don't be sorry. Just be glad you have a dad *and* a mom . . . and the twins. And grandparents who are part of your life. Not everyone has that."

"You're so right." Emma stopped herself before saying, "I'm sorry" again. Instead, she said, "Thanks for the reminder."

"Dad and I do just fine. He does a great job at being my dad and filling in as Mom." Chloe giggled. "But he struggles with . . . you know . . . the girl stuff."

"I get that," Emma said. An uncomfortable laugh sneaked out. "My dad gets weirded out by girl stuff too."

Again, quiet overtook the pair. And again, it was Chloe who broke the silence. "By the way, I signed us up for auditions for the musical. I put you down for the lead, of course. And I'm going to try out for the sidekick. Kind of fitting, right?"

Emma hesitated over what she was about to say. "I may skip the musical this year."

"What?" Chloe stopped walking. "You've been talking about it ever since they announced it. You've been in every performance since like third grade. What's up?"

Emma turned to face her friend. *Tell her* came a voice from within that was not her own. Emma wanted to do just that, but how?

"It's hard to explain. I don't fully understand it myself." Emma struggled as her mind fumbled for words, words that Chloe would accept and that wouldn't sound deranged. At last, a partial thought formed, and she opened her mouth. "Ah—"

"Morning, ladies," interrupted a male voice from behind. Emma spun around. It was Lane. He said this every morning. Though directing his words at both girls, he always looked at Chloe. But Chloe never noticed. Nor did she notice Joshua standing next to him.

Why does Chloe have two guys who like her, and I have none? Though Emma didn't need a boyfriend, it would be nice for her to have a guy to share life with. Yet Emma wasn't sure if the stirring in her soul left any room for such feelings. She'd already pushed aside the musical for the sake of the Sovereign. Would she need to give up romance too? Would this be another casualty as she pursued her growing faith? A faith that she still didn't understand.

Though she dreamed of one day having a family, Emma now wondered if the Sovereign would demand she remain single. These thoughts flooded her mind throughout the school day as she struggled to focus on her classes.

Just how much will I need to give up for the Sovereign?

5

EMMA'S CREW

After school, Emma and Chloe waited for the rest of the group to arrive before heading home.

"I can't stop thinking about Mrs. Butler," Chloe said. "Will we ever see her again?"

Emma's mind thought about their missing religion teacher too. In her spirit, Emma sensed they would see Mrs. Butler again, but how could Emma explain this supernatural knowledge to her best friend?

Chloe continued. "Have you ever heard of anyone arrested for heresy and inciting sedition who's ever come back from retraining?"

"It's just a rumor."

"But everyone knows that's what happened."

"Let's focus on what we know—you and I," Emma said. "Just the facts."

Chloe scrunched up her face as she thought. At last, she lit up. "We know Principal Johnson had to cover Mrs. Butler's first hour class until they could find an emergency sub."

"That's one." Emma held up her index finger. "And two, we know her car was in the school parking lot after everyone else had left."

"And it sat there for a week and then disappeared, but no one has seen her since." Chloe held up three fingers.

"We don't know that last part as fact," Emma said. "It's just that no one *we* know has seen her. Maybe other people have."

"Still, the only reasonable conclusion is that she was arrested and sent for retraining."

Emma shook her head. "Maybe she had a medical emergency and is in the hospital . . . or a family crisis and had to leave."

Chloe raised her eyebrows. "Without her car?"

"Maybe she had car trouble."

"Or maybe they arrested her for heresy and inciting sedition. Then sent her away for retraining."

Emma sighed. "Perhaps."

The pair went silent as they waited.

Joshua arrived first, and soon everyone else was there. Emma headed out with her flock of friends in tow, a precaution that had developed this year, intensified by the rumor of Mrs. Butler's arrest.

Why they looked to Emma as their leader, she didn't know. She felt unworthy, yet she accepted their esteem as somehow inevitable. The Sovereign was at work deep inside her spirit. This much was clear. *Could this troupe somehow sense it,* Emma wondered, *following me for a reason they didn't understand?*

Ever since the High Priest had died last year without a successor, as his second-in-command at the Temple, His Royal Eminence had assumed all the High Priest's duties. Though lacking the training to be a priest, let alone the birthright to be High Priest, he inserted himself into that role. The people accepted him without question.

Shortly after His Royal Eminence rose to power at the Temple, the state's SWAT division began rounding up people they labeled as heretics. Was there a connection? The Prime Minister, who was supposed to serve at the High Priest's behest, now seemed intent on opposing the Temple her office was intended to serve.

Rumors of arrests came more frequently, while no one seemed to know where the people went, or if they'd ever return. Traveling in groups seemed wise, at least until things calmed down.

Still, life was good for Emma, at least mostly so. The gentle sun warmed her face. It was easy to dismiss the evil that had emerged in this leadership vacuum and assume she and those she loved were safe.

Interrupting her bliss came the siren of a SWAT team. Each time she heard its warning, the eerie wail triggered an involuntary shudder. The idea of being rounded up with the deviants bound for retraining produced fear in everyone.

The pulsating alert grew closer, and the convoy screeched to a halt next to Emma's group. She tensed. Instinctively, the students stepped back from the curb and pressed against the bricks of the building behind them.

Donned in full combat gear, the force exited their vehicles. They headed right toward Emma, but Joshua stepped in front of her. The poor guy shrieked as a SWAT team member jammed a cattle prod into his side. Joshua collapsed to the ground, writhing in pain. The soldier sneered with delight.

Two of the militia grabbed his legs and dragged him to their police van.

"Stop!" Emma screamed as she took a step toward Joshua. "He's done nothing wrong." Her ill-timed words escaped her mouth before she could corral them.

"This miscreant requires retraining," the militia's leader said.

Outfitted as a captain, his uniform gave his name, Hernandez. Emma committed the name and face to memory.

"His recent online activities suggest he's a dangerous heretic and a threat to society," the captain continued. "We also round up troublemakers. Care to join him?"

Emma opened her mouth but shook her head instead. Her mind told her to back away, but her body remained frozen with fear. Another soldier slapped her cheek—hard. His black leather glove smacked against her soft, innocent skin.

Emma gasped and tried to suck in a breath, but she couldn't when he thrust the butt of his gun into her gut. As she doubled over, he shoved her away. She fell backward to the ground with a thud, her head smacking the sidewalk with a sickening crack.

Another soldier laughed. He thrust his cattle

prod toward her face. It stopped only inches from her brow.

"Better watch out, missy," Hernandez said. "Or you'll be next."

As the squad peeled away in their caravan, a dazed Emma expected everyone to gather around her to help. But most of the troupe scattered, and the rest stepped back. In rapid succession, they each shook their heads and scurried away. Only Chloe remained.

The diminutive girl cast a quick glance up and down the street. Only then did she step toward Emma. She bent down and extended her hand. "You must be more careful," she whispered. "Can you get up?"

"Think so."

Chloe helped Emma to rise and steady her quaking body. Then Chloe spun on her heel and sped off, leaving Emma alone—and terrified.

Emma asked the Sovereign for protection. That was her only hope if she had any chance of making it home tonight. Of that, she was sure.

6

___

A ONE-WORD PRAYER

Though always warned to keep to main roads, Emma feared the SWAT team might circle back and arrest her too. This meant that staying where she was or moving along this well-traveled route were both unwise choices.

Yet the alleys carried a different peril. Danger awaited her there, as her parents had warned her over the years. She had but two options: bad and worse.

Emma waited for the Sovereign to give direction. Nothing happened. She sucked in a desperate gulp of air and rasped an imperative plea, a one-word prayer. "Please." Though Emma only had a childlike belief in the Sovereign, her faith had been growing. She knew she could trust the Almighty to guide her to make the right decisions on how to get home.

That's when Emma noticed the homeless man —the one she had given money to yesterday— standing across the street. He raised his arm and pointed an emphatic finger behind her. She glanced at an alley. Turning back to the man, her face asked an unspoken question. He nodded and pointed again with greater intention.

Take the alley. The command came not from the man but from her own head. Yet it wasn't her voice, and those weren't her words. They originated from a different place. Whether that was from far away or deep inside, she didn't know.

Move! This time the surreal command came with increased clarity. Frozen with indecision, Emma remained immobile until a distant siren urged her to move. She spun around and sprinted to the alley.

"Protect me, Sovereign." Her whispered prayer rasped out over her lips. As she continued her appeal, words spurted out between sucking in deep breaths of oxygen as she pressed to run as fast as she could, her knapsack bouncing on her back with each step.

Before her, two homeless women fought over a

bright, satin scarf. Emma offered them a wide berth as she rushed past, but they gave her no notice, as if they couldn't see her. She continued for three more blocks, running full out. Not used to intense physical activity, she stopped and bent down. Resting her hands on her knees, she sucked in deep gulps of air. Her head pounded where it had struck the sidewalk. Her heart thumped and her stomach roiled. Bile rose in her throat.

Left, said the ethereal voice inside her head.

Left didn't look safe, so Emma glanced right. That was the better path, guiding her toward a not-as-risky part of the city.

Move! came the voice again.

Emma obeyed and turned left. She dared not run, fearing she'd throw up. But she did jog. She hadn't gone twenty feet when a single gunshot echoed from behind on the route she almost took. Emma shifted into high gear.

Her path took her toward a man and woman arguing. Uncertain what to do, Emma slowed her pace.

The woman, scantily dressed and wearing way too much makeup, stared in a standoff with the man. He wore a black trench coat and towered over the woman by at least a foot. She glared daggers up at him, and he responded with furled brows of disdain.

"You forget who's in charge." The man stated this as fact and with a sneer. He slapped the woman hard on her face. At the resounding smack of skin striking skin, Emma brought a cautious hand to her own wounded cheek. It throbbed, almost as intense as her pounding head. *Did the SWAT soldier break my cheekbone?*

"Now get back to work!" the man said to his charge.

Curiously, neither of them noticed Emma as she slid by.

The voice of the Sovereign, as if implanting words in her mind, had guided her well so far. Emma resolved to stay on this questionable path until instructed otherwise. A couple of blocks ahead, two men argued. One carried a bottle wrapped in a paper bag. The other man wanted it.

Now, with full confidence in the Sovereign's protection, Emma moved forward without breaking stride. As she approached the two men, they came together to exchange blows and then pulled apart. Emma ran between them, as if the sea had parted.

Once she passed, she heard the fight resume, and it wasn't long before glass shattered.

Despite an increasing dizziness, she moved forward at a hurried yet sustainable pace. Bringing her hand to the back of her head, she encountered a warm ooze. She pulled her hand away to discover her fingers covered with blood. She couldn't deal with that now. She had to get home first.

Aside from suspecting that her path headed in the general direction of her house, Emma had no idea where she was. Dusk descended. She recognized no landmarks. The few street signs she could make out carried unfamiliar names.

But the Sovereign continued to guide her. *Left, right,* or *straight.* Each instruction came just as Emma needed it. She now obeyed every command without hesitation. Sometimes additional instructions told her *fast, slow,* or even *stop.* She had faith that each one steered her away from or around some life-threatening danger, even as dusk yielded to dark.

At last, she found herself on a familiar road. She knew the way home. Yet the Sovereign guided her along a roundabout route, taking her to the side door of her home. She slipped into the house unnoticed and crept with quiet intention to the bathroom. She ducked inside and eased the door shut with a click.

Only now did she notice the intense, pounding throb pulsating against her temples.

7

———

A CLOSE CALL

mma's family held hands around the dinner table and thanked the Sovereign for their food. At the "amen," each one opened their eyes. That's when Emma's mom scrutinized her face.

"Is that a bruise on your cheek?"

Emma squirmed. "Silly me. I wasn't looking where I was going and walked into a door." She forced out a giggle but was sure it sounded phony.

Her dad accepted her explanation with a nod, but her mom raised an eyebrow.

Eager to avoid further interrogation, Emma changed the subject. "Since the High Priest died without an heir, why can't they just appoint someone?"

"That's a question most have asked," her mom said, while still studying Emma's face.

"Many have tried to ascend to the position and failed," her dad added.

"Why?" Emma knew the answer, but she needed to keep this conversation going if she hoped to avoid explaining the bruise on her cheek, as well as revealing the tenderness of her tummy and the oozing wound hiding beneath her hair.

"They enter the Temple on the eve of the full moon," her dad said. "But by morning, they're dead. The Sovereign rejected each one—everyone who's tried."

"Not everyone dies," her mom corrected. "A few have emerged in the early morning light, but they're dazed and babbling. They're picked up by a SWAT team. We're told it's for their own protection."

"Surely someone with a pure heart who understands the Sovereign's perspective could become the new High Priest." Emma blurted her words without thinking, but she wondered if she might be right.

Her parents both shook their heads, and her two younger siblings stared at her with wide-eyed astonishment.

"We must be missing something," Emma

thought aloud. "Until recently, we always had a continuous line of High Priests, and the Sovereign has always taken care of us. Now we have no High Priest to guide us and keep the government in check. They're out of control. We're no longer safe and are subject to arrest at any moment."

Her parents' concerned glances confirmed she shouldn't have said that last sentence. She stretched out her leg underneath the table and kicked the side of Hailey's shin.

The young girl turned to glare at Brayden. "Knock it off, jerk!"

The noise that followed confirmed kicking between the twins. Emma willed her lips to stay immobile to suppress the grin that threatened to erupt.

Now focusing on separating their squabbling children, her parents forgot Emma's mention of government corruption, fear for personal safety, and threats of arrest. From now on, she'd need to guard what she said if she hoped to obey the growing urgency in her soul to act.

8

CRAZY OR CONSECRATED?

That night, Emma tossed in her bed. Her body ached; her mind knotted with confusion. Yet it was what had happened to Joshua that caused her primary disquiet.

She played and replayed countless ideas of what she could do to free him, along with all the other wrongly incarcerated people. She imagined herself marching up to the detention center and demanding the release of Joshua and all the religious prisoners. There'd be media coverage, a throng of like-minded protesters, and a trembling administrator eager to comply. She'd repeat this at each facility until the government caved in and released everyone across the country.

Emma smiled at the image of her powerful and

effective crusade but shook her head at how unrealistic it was. Though she fancied herself as a dynamic woman with the ability to do anything, she was just an average teenager, not even old enough to drive.

She shook these intriguing thoughts from her mind. Yet, another one rushed in to replace it.

This time Emma stood boldly in front of the Senate, testifying of the atrocities placed on an innocent—and harmless—sliver of the population. She'd demand the immediate release of everyone illegally detained and the prosecution of those who orchestrated it.

With her task complete, she'd exit the chamber to a cacophony of camera clicks, a surge of reporters throwing questions at her as they thrust microphones in her face, and the zoomed-in attention of video cameras from every major media outlet.

If only reality could match her imagination. She willed herself to stop these senseless fantasies and go to sleep. To distract herself, she considered a perplexing extra credit algebra problem.

The diversion did the trick. For a while.

At 3:00 a.m. she woke, shivering from the cold sweat that soaked her nightgown. Her thoughts jumped back to the SWAT team dragging off Joshua. It could have just as easily been her. She sensed it should have been. Hernandez had headed right toward her.

She had to do something. Though Joshua's presence confused her, she'd grown used to him hanging around.

Another fanciful rescue scenario emerged. This time she wore black. It was the middle of the night. She embarked on a clandestine attempt to infiltrate the prison, find Joshua and the other prisoners there for retraining, and free them all. But that would only address one prison. What about all the other detention centers across the country?

Transportation would be a huge problem. Never mind that she had neither the skill nor the ability to carry out such a bold mission. Though these types of fanciful stories played well on TV and in movies, they were unrealistic for a fifteen-year-old who used her mind—not special ops skills—to solve problems.

Speaking of problems, she forced herself to return to the unfinished algebra challenge. She drifted back to sleep while wondering if she had an overactive imagination or had received divine—albeit confusing—inspiration.

As the morning light poked its way into her bedroom, her essence hovered in that fuzzy but somewhat familiar place, teetering between physical reality and the spiritual realm. Another fanciful scenario emerged. Her spirit watched her body march up to the Temple as dusk descended. She'd wait inside to connect with the Sovereign and implore the Almighty for relief. If she died trying—like most everyone who had preceded her—at least she would have tried. Maybe her death could serve as a catalyst for change.

But did she even have the nerve to go to the Temple? And if she showed up, would the priests let her stay through the night? They'd surely look down on her for being young and female.

Do it, that surreal voice in her head said. It wasn't audible; it was otherworldly. Though hearing disembodied speech didn't happen often for Emma—at least not until yesterday—she had received divine direction a few times in the past. She hadn't dared tell anyone because her mom had said normal people couldn't hear from the Sovereign. Emma feared these experiences might mean she was crazy—or consecrated. She wasn't sure which answer troubled her more.

Spending the night in the Temple was something she could do. But did she have enough courage to try? Was she willing to die for this cause?

The wrongly imprisoned innocents were not the real problem; they were merely the result. The underlying issue was the lack of a High Priest to guide the people and place a needed check on government overreach from the Prime Minister and her questionable reassignment of the SWAT squads. What the people needed most was to reconnect with the Sovereign, and that required a High Priest, someone who would restore right worship.

Pushing slumber aside and forcing her complete self to return to her present reality, Emma opened her eyes to greet the dawn. Once again grounded in the physical realm, she prepared to embrace the day and all its potential.

Refusing to let yesterday's trauma dictate today, she stumbled out of bed, dressed as fast as her sore body permitted, and hastened down the stairs—taking two steps at a time—eager to embrace her groggy family.

9

———

AN EARLY START

Emma bounded into the kitchen. "I'm getting an early start on my day." She announced this with a perkiness she seldom felt when first rising and certainly not after this weirdest-of-all night that she'd just experienced.

She paused and gathered her siblings in her arms and gave each a quick kiss on their forehead before they could squirm away. Next, she hugged her dad with tight intention and then kissed her mom last. "I love you all . . . so very much."

Her mom frowned. "Emma . . . is everything okay?"

"Couldn't be better . . . See you at dinner." At least she hoped so.

Emma scooted out, leaving her perplexed

family in her wake. She took the back way to Chloe's house, desperate to avoid any morning patrols, especially the SWAT captain, Hernandez, who was probably keeping a watch out for her.

As Emma worked her way through backyards and weaved around fences, she wondered if her best friend would even talk to her after yesterday's ordeal. But before Emma could knock on Chloe's back door, it opened a crack. A hand shot out and jerked her inside.

Chloe wrapped her arms around Emma, pulling her close as she shut the door with her foot. "So sorry about yesterday. Shouldn't have ditched. Please forgive."

Chloe's words relieved Emma. "No problem. We're all good."

Chloe stared at Emma's cheek. "Does it hurt much?" She reached for it but didn't touch it.

"Not as much as my stomach. But I'm more concerned about my head."

Chloe's gaze shifted to the top of Emma's head.

"It's in the back. It bled a lot. I cleaned it up the best I could without being able to see what I was doing. I couldn't very well ask Mom to look at it. Too many questions."

"Where is it?"

Emma guided Chloe's hovering hand from over her cheek to the back of her head, directing her friend's hand close to the tender area.

"Take a seat. Let me have a peek."

Emma complied. Chloe's gentle touch combed through Emma's hair to assess the damage. "You got it cleaned up pretty well, but you need stitches."

"I can't go to my parents or the school nurse. There'd be questions and it would cause more problems than I already have. Can you do it?"

"No way! Just because I took a first aid class doesn't mean I'm prepared—or willing—to stick a needle in your head."

"Then ask the Sovereign to heal me." Emma said this as though it was both normal and easy, even though she'd never heard of such a thing occurring. At least not anymore.

"What?"

"Supernatural healings occur in the Holy Text. Why can't they happen today?"

"What do you know about the Holy Text?" Chloe asked in disbelief.

"I've been studying it. Every night before bed. At least an hour, sometimes two."

"Seriously?"

"If you won't do it, I will. Guide me to where I need stitches." Emma extended her index finger.

Chloe hesitated but moved Emma's hand toward the open wound.

"Sovereign Lord, I don't know how to do this or what to say, but I believe you can heal my head just like in the Holy Text. May it be so." Emma lifted her finger.

Chloe gasped. "The wound is closing! I can't believe it . . . The blotchiness is going away . . . You don't need stitches anymore . . . I doubt thcrc'll even be a scar. How in the world did you do that?"

"I didn't. The Sovereign did. All it takes is a tiny bit of faith, even as small as a grain of salt."

"I don't even have that much."

"But you can . . . you will."

Chloe opened her mouth to say something but stopped when Emma's phone vibrated.

Emma looked at the screen and drew in a slow breath. "It's a text from Mom. She says the police are looking for me and have a few questions. She wants me to come home to straighten everything out."

"Will you?"

"Not if I want to stay out of jail and avoid

retraining. I'm not going to school either. I need to do some research."

"About what?"

"I don't remember the Holy Text ever talking about approaching the Sovereign on a full moon. What if everyone's been doing it wrong? I need to find a new way, the right way."

Chloe stood still and stared.

"You go to school like normal," Emma said. "If anyone asks, you haven't seen me today. Got it?"

"Got it!"

Emma scooted out the back door. *Is it wrong for me to ask Chloe to lie?*

10

GABE

Sequestered in a back corner of the public library where she could hide what she was doing, Emma searched for answers. With dozens of religious books surrounding her, and aided by an online search, she all but confirmed there was no record of needing to seek the Sovereign on a full moon. But she could find no instructions for the proper time either. She also didn't discover any passages in the library's copy of the Holy Text about how to replace a High Priest who died without an heir.

Having missed breakfast and now working through lunch, Emma's stomach rumbled with discontent. But her food fast wasn't only practical; it seemed spiritual too. Clarity emerged. A plan took shape.

If everyone had approached the Almighty on a full moon and failed, why not do the opposite and try a new moon instead? That would be in seven days. This would give her one week to prepare, even though the last four hours of research had given her no insight into what to do.

Emma lowered her head to rest on the open Holy Text in front of her. She closed her eyes. *Sovereign Lord,* she prayed with silent words. *Show me what to do.*

She wondered if her petition should be more elegant and longer, but at least it came from her heart.

"Don't be afraid, my child," whispered a man's voice from behind her.

Alarmed, Emma sat up. Her body tensed. She held her breath, half expecting to feel a knife plunge into her back. Yet the other half of her sensed she was quite safe.

"Please forgive my intrusion. I didn't mean to startle you." Arriving at the same time as his words came the same nauseating stench from the other day. It wafted to Emma's nose and assaulted her sense of smell.

Her shoulders dropped as she exhaled in relief. It was the homeless man. She didn't even need to turn around to check.

"May I join you?"

Emma didn't answer, for his voice was already moving closer. He rounded the table and sat facing her.

Oh, Sovereign. He really stinks. Keep me from puking.

"Let me apologize for my odiferous emanations. Oh, what I wouldn't give for a hot shower and clean clothes." He gave a dismissive wave with the back of his hand.

The smell vanished. Emma took a deep breath. "How did you do that?"

"The how matters not, only that I did. If you'd like, one day I can teach you." His eyes twinkled. "Or do you prefer the odor to return?"

"Please, no! I couldn't deal with it."

"With the Sovereign's help, you can deal with anything. Of that I know with all surety."

Emma dismissed his suggestion. It was easier to ignore his words than figure out what he meant. "Who are you, anyway?"

"Here, I'm known as Gabe."

"As in Gabriel? Like in the Holy Text?"

"Don't be fanciful, my dear child, trying to connect dots that don't warrant a connection."

"I was just wondering—"

"Sir, I need to ask you to leave." Even though Emma no longer smelled Gabe, the woman scrunched up her nose in disgust and flapped a futile hand in front of it. She wore her hair pulled back into a bun. A white cardigan sweater draped over her shoulders, and half-glasses hung from her neck by a chain. "You can stay," the librarian said to Emma.

"He has as much right to be here as I do." There she went again, speaking without thinking. Emma stood up and locked eyes with the librarian. Why did she do this, acting without considering the consequences? "He's helping me with my studies." Emma gestured at the books in front of her.

"Shouldn't you be in school?"

Busted. Emma's mind swirled in search of a response. "I'm working on a . . . special assignment." She hoped this would placate the distrustful librarian and avoid spinning a lie, which the Holy Text forbade.

The librarian hesitated. "We don't want another incident. Please keep the noise down and try not to scare away the other patrons." The librarian spun around and stomped off.

"Now, where were we?" Gabe rubbed his bearded chin. "Ah, yes. It's good to wonder, to ask questions."

"Do you have any family you could live with?" Emma studied his face, waiting for a reaction.

"A son, but we're estranged." Gabe looked away. When his gaze returned, his eyes glistened. "He refuses to speak to me."

"The Holy Text says, 'Blessed are those who seek restoration.' Have you tried that?"

"Many times," the old man said. "I'm now following the command to 'live at peace with all people to the degree possible.' Keeping my distance is the best way I know to give him peace."

"What about other relatives?" Emma wasn't sure if she should continue probing, but the questions kept popping out.

"My son has a daughter. About your age. Though I've seen her from afar, I doubt she has any knowledge of my existence."

"What in the world happened?" Emma's impertinent questions continued to flow, as if she had no control over them.

"Unwise decisions and numerous indiscretions

litter my past. My son has every reason to distance himself and every reason to prohibit my grand-daughter from having any interaction with me."

"But—"

"But we shouldn't waste what precious time we have today dwelling on my past." Gabe pawed at his misty eyes. "Let us address the more pressing questions you have about the present." Gabe's gentle voice overflowed with compassion. He was a good man. She would do well to listen to him.

"I've been reading the Holy Text," Emma whispered. "But many parts confuse me."

"The Sovereign adores those who search for truth in Scripture."

"I study it every night." Emma glanced around to make sure no one could hear her. "I listen to my heart and make notes in my journal."

"What if it isn't your heart speaking to you, but the Sovereign?"

Emma had never considered this. "Then why am I still confused?"

"In our present, physical reality," Gabe said, "we will never ascertain all we desire to compre-hend and satiate our quest for more. But that doesn't imply we shouldn't seek to discern truth."

"I want to ask the Sovereign to send us a new

High Priest, but I haven't figured out the right way to do it—at least not yet."

"May I?" Gabe tipped his head toward the Holy Text. Emma had hoped no one could see it lying open on the table, but he did.

"Please."

He stretched out his gnarled finger. With a gentleness that shocked Emma, he paged forward in the book, leaving it facing her and upside down to him. After four or five tender flips of his finger, he stopped. He squinted. "Second column, third line. Read. Aloud."

Emma pulled the sacred book closer and read softly. She didn't want to incur the librarian's wrath or call attention to what she was reading. "Approach the Sovereign with a pure heart and live; those with selfish intent will perish—be it in body or in spirit."

She gasped. "Is that why everyone who's tried has died or gone crazy?"

"You already know the answer to your query, so why seek confirmation from me?"

"You mean the answer is a pure heart? But how can anyone have a pure heart in today's crazy world?"

"Asking suggests you are already on your way,"

Gabe said. "The rest is a step of faith."

"I have so little."

"We all need more faith, my child. But I sense you have enough to move forward."

"I'm just a girl. Looking for answers. You call me a child, and what little faith I have is like that of a child."

"A childlike faith is key." Gabe stroked his scraggly beard. The gesture made him seem even wiser. "The Sovereign's Divine Spirit within you shines bright, brighter than any I've seen in many a decade."

Emma glanced down, half expecting to see a glow emanating from her chest. She saw nothing.

"We can only see the aura of a person's spirit in the supernatural realm. It doesn't exist in the physical."

"We?"

"All people have access to the power of the spiritual realm," Gabe said. "It's just that most aren't aware of it, and few even try to access it."

"All people? Even me?"

"Especially you."

"You act as though I'm someone I'm not." These words did not come out as Emma normally spoke. They sounded more like Gabe. *Is he rubbing off on me?*

"Not only does your spirit shine bright, but it's a pure, white light."

"Does that mean my heart is pure?" Desperate, Emma needed Gabe to confirm that it was. Yet at the same time, she feared he would.

"Yes, my child." Gabe's face lit up with a sudden realization. He leaned forward. "Are you the One?" His question was earnest.

"Don't be silly. Of course not."

"But your glow. It's so bright," Gabe said. "Surely you are the One."

"Surely, I am *not*." Emma mimicked Gabe to make her point, yet the words sounded funny coming from her mouth.

"Present your hand to me," the wise man said.

Emma extended her arm as if to shake hands.

"The other one."

Emma withdrew her right hand as she extended her left. It felt awkward.

Instead of a clumsy handshake, as Emma expected, Gabe gave her another command. "Rotate ninety degrees. Palm up."

Emma complied.

"Open your spirit to seek truth." Gabe cradled

the underside of her hand with his own and brought his other hand to rest on top of hers.

A tingle flowed into her hand from his, bringing with it an overwhelming sense of peace. Her mind spun, and she let it go where it wished. She perceived her spirit communicating with his on a higher plane, one she had never experienced but suspected existed, nonetheless.

With eyes closed tight like a vise, Gabe's lips moved, but no sound came out. Faster and faster his lips contorted until a breathy rasp emerged. It sounded like a language, but not one Emma had ever heard.

Gabe's eyes popped wide open. He pulled back his hands with a jerk. "Inconceivable! How could I have made such a grievous error? You are *not* the One." He shook his head with disbelief. "But I sense you are remarkably close to the person who will be."

Emma didn't know if this should relieve or disappoint her.

"I must seek the Sovereign on this for additional clarity." Gabe again stroked his unkempt beard.

But Emma didn't want to consider what he said. At least, not right now. She sought a diversion and glanced at the passage in the Holy Text. "I'm trying to memorize key passages, but this one is hard to understand."

"Read the section again," he whispered.

Emma read the passage again, this time with more confidence but not more volume. "Approach the Sovereign with a pure heart and live; those with selfish intent will perish—be it in body or in spirit."

"Visualize the words on the page. See them in your head and imprint them in your heart." Gabe stretched out his arm toward Emma's head, palm open and facing her. "May I?"

Emma wasn't sure what he was asking, but she knew the correct answer. "Yes."

He rested his palm on the top of her head. Warmth flowed from his touch. A calm washed over her. Every muscle in her body relaxed.

"Close your eyes and see the Text in your mind. Say the words. Implant them into your soul." Gabe slid his hand to the back of her head. Applying the gentlest of touches, he guided her head down. Her forehead landed on the open pages of the sacred book. "Meditate on these words and you will know what to do." He lifted his hand from her head, but the warmth remained.

Approach the Sovereign with a pure heart and live. Emma breathed in. She breathed out. She repeated the passage and let it become part of her, opening her spirit to receive its wisdom.

At last, she understood. She was making this much harder than it needed to be. It wasn't an issue of a full moon or a new moon. It was as simple as the Holy Text said. "Approach the Sovereign with a pure heart and live."

"Got it!" She jerked her head up, expecting to see approval in Gabe's eyes, but he was gone.

11

SANCTUARY

Emma's vibrating phone interrupted her deliberation on what to do next. It was a text from Chloe. "The cops are looking for you at school. I heard them say they've requested permission from their boss to track your phone."

Emma immediately knew just what to do.

Even though her fear implored her to run, she tapped her theater training to play the role of a carefree teen. She stood and forced herself to move with a casual indifference. Leaving the table and its array of books, she headed toward the library's exit. On her way out, she slid her cell phone into the book return slot.

Then she strolled away, as if she didn't have a

single care. She passed a woman who stopped short and stared. The woman whispered to her companion. "Isn't that the girl on TV?"

"I don't think so," her friend said. "I'm sure they would have arrested her by now."

Without breaking stride, Emma kept up her intentional pace. She tried not to dwell on their comments. New moon or not, tonight she would seek the Sovereign and implore her Lord to appoint a new High Priest who could restore order. First, she needed to set things right with those she cared about—in case she failed.

To do so, she needed to get to school, while avoiding public transportation and security cams. Her journey could take hours on foot.

Sovereign, show me which path to take.

Hearing nothing, Emma took a tentative step toward the school.

Two blocks and then turn left, said the Sovereign. Emma quickened her pace on that course.

The Sovereign's promptings flowed into her receptive mind. That strange, yet unmistakable, voice began directing her steps, just like yesterday. This time, Emma obeyed each instruction without hesitation. In a couple of hours, she neared the school but stopped short.

Police cars and SWAT vehicles filled the parking lot. Some officers stood still and talked on their radios. Others darted around as if on some frantic mission but with no purpose she could see. In the middle of the commotion stood Captain Hernandez, barking out orders.

Emma eased into a clump of bushes at the nearest house, allowing them to surround her and hide her presence. From there, she could monitor the police activity at a safe distance.

As she waited for the police to leave, she sat on the ground and wrote a note to her parents, telling them she loved them, what she was doing, and why. She told them to be happy for her, whatever the outcome.

Next was a note to Chloe.

You're my best friend, but I haven't been as good of a friend to you. I've learned so much studying the Holy Text—about the Sovereign, about faith, about living. But I never told you. I'm so sorry I kept the most important part of my life a secret.

In my bedroom, between the springs and mattress of my bed, I have a notebook full of what I've learned. I want you to have it. It will guide you in how to develop your faith.

I'm going to the Temple to seek the Sovereign and ask for a new High Priest to deliver us. If I die trying, I'm okay with that because I believe I'm here for such a time as this.

I also have a note for my parents. If I don't make it back, please give it to them. I love you and wish we had more time. There's so much more I want to share.

Emma fashioned a makeshift envelope out of another sheet of paper and shoved both notes inside. As she finished, some of the police cars and SWAT vehicles peeled away, perhaps heading to the library where she had left her phone. But some remained, so Emma could do nothing but stay put until they left.

Growing more impatient as each second passed, she waited for the remaining vehicles to depart, but they didn't. She watched Chloe leave for the day with their group—minus her and Joshua—but she saw no safe way to connect with her friend and give her the letters without risking arrest.

Should she abandon her plan to share what might be her last words with her family and her best friend so she could head straight to the Temple? Emma struggled with indecision. When she considered delaying her mission for one day, a strange peace enveloped her.

It was the Sovereign's approval to a revised schedule. *Your letters are important. You must deliver them.*

But what to do? *Should I wait until tomorrow for a chance to give Chloe both letters?*

Yes! came the Sovereign's immediate reply.

What should I do until then?

This time the Sovereign was silent.

Show me what to do, Emma begged.

Before her was the school. She considered places on the grounds where she might hide for the night, but it didn't seem like a smart move. This was confirmed when Gabe walked from around the other side of the building. He stopped by the walk leading up to the school's main entrance and looked her way. He crossed his arms and shook his head.

Thank you, Sovereign.

Behind her sat the subdivision, but no solutions

presented themselves there either. Hunched over, Emma crept along the hedge that surrounded the school. Her heart thumped with worry over what to do. Hands shaking, she shoved branches aside as she pressed forward with purpose but no destination. Her eyes scanned each house, searching for safety, praying for direction. Nothing. Emma pressed on, walking through the backyards of one home after another.

After a dozen or so houses, she came upon one yard with several old oak trees. The largest supported a playhouse. It was just like in her vision. It was accessible yet secluded enough to afford her the protection she sought. She paused and opened her mind to hear.

Sanctuary, the Sovereign said.

Emma huddled in the shadows until dusk. She crept toward the tree house's ladder and scampered up. She poked her head through the opening in the floor to see a large platform with a well-constructed roof and sturdy walls. Each side had a window. One offered her a clear view of the school.

Thank you, Sovereign, Emma prayed. *This is perfect.*

12

SARAH

I f only she had something to eat and a blanket to ward off the evening's chill. To distract herself from what she didn't have, Emma focused her attention on recalling passages from the Holy Text. These comforted her and filled her with peace. In her spirit, she reached out to the Sovereign.

"Emma," came an imperative whisper.

Was she dreaming, or was it real?

"Emma," came the whisper again. "I have food."

The voice came from below. Emma poked her head out with care and looked down. There stood a young girl, probably in middle school. She held a basket in her hand. The girl's face brightened. She held up the container. "Hungry?"

Emma nodded but realized the girl wouldn't be able to see. "Yes," Emma whispered back.

"There's a rope with a hook on the end. Lower it."

Emma did, and the girl put the basket on the hook. Emma drew the rope up. As she did, the savory smell of a meaty stew filled her nostrils with expectation. Her stomach rumbled its anticipation. She licked her lips.

Once she secured the basket and its bounty, Emma poked her head out to whisper thanks.

But before she could, the girl spoke. "I also have a sleeping bag. Lower the rope again."

Emma complied, and she soon hauled up a quilted sleeping bag. She looked down to say thanks, but the girl was already climbing the ladder.

A head poked into Emma's sanctuary. The girl looked familiar, with large, captivating brown eyes and a crooked grin. She was tall for her age. "Mom thought you might be hungry."

"I haven't eaten all day."

"She saw you out back when she was doing dishes and said, 'We have to help Emma.'"

"How do you know my name?"

"By now, everyone does. Your picture is plastered all over the internet."

Emma gasped. "Why?"

"You stood up for Joshua when they arrested him. Everyone's calling you a hero, and now the cops are out to get you. My name's Sarah, by the way. We wanted to invite you in for a proper meal and warm bed, but our house isn't safe. The cops keep stopping by to see if we've heard from you."

"Why would I contact you?" Emma shook her head as if that would help make sense of the situation. "I don't even know your family."

"Because they think you and Joshua are close. His social media profile lists you as a friend."

"I have hundreds of friends on social media."

"Joshua only has three," Sarah said with a giggle. "Besides, he likes you."

"How do you know that?"

"He's my brother, silly."

That's why the girl looked so familiar. "Got it." Emma's mind churned through this revelation. "So . . . since he lives so close to school, why does he walk home with me every day?"

"To make sure you're safe. Besides, he really likes you. I just told you that, remember? Do you like him?"

"I'm not sure." Emma considered Joshua from a fresh perspective. "To be honest, he sometimes bugs me. He's always hovering."

"Yeah, he can be annoying. But I do love him. Give him a chance when he gets out. We're praying for his release."

"Me too," Emma said. Though it made little sense, she believed the Sovereign would answer their prayers.

"But you have a plan, too, don't you?" Sarah asked, wide-eyed with expectation.

"I guess I do, but it's a long shot. Praying is probably better."

Sarah sat down and unpacked the food from the basket. She kept up an unfiltered, yet engaging, monologue as Emma wolfed down the tasty meal. But she was hungry enough that she'd have enjoyed just about anything.

As Emma swallowed the last of her supper, Sarah unrolled the sleeping bag. "Joshua and I used to sleep up here sometimes, but now he says I'm forbidden. Still, it was great fun while it lasted."

Emma gave Sarah an appreciative hug. "Tell your mom thanks."

"Will do." Sarah headed to the ladder but stopped. "Almost forgot. Dad said we'd keep the back door unlocked in case you need to use the bathroom. But we can't leave the lights on because it might attract attention. The bathroom is to the right when you get in." Sarah descended the ladder and scurried toward the house.

Emma snuggled into the sleeping bag and whispered her thanks to the Sovereign.

13

RUBY RED

Faint rays of the morning dawn bathed the tree house with a comforting calm. Emma stretched and gave a contented moan. But she sensed she wasn't alone. She rolled over, and there was Gabe sitting on the far side of the tree house. Disturbing? Yes. Scary? No.

Sitting cross-legged on the floor, he rested his hands on his thighs, palms up as if expecting to receive something. His eyes remained closed as his lips twisted in rapid movement. A low rasp leaked out, just as before.

She smiled. "A bit creepy, old man."

Gabe's eyes popped open. "My apologies, dear child. I'm preparing for the day that awaits us. Though the Holy Text doesn't specify it, I suspect proximity stands as a wise prerequisite to include you in my petition for protection."

Emma rubbed the sleep from her eyes, wiped her lips to rid them of the possibility of drool, and sat up. She combed through her hair with her fingers to corral its morning chaos. She clutched the sleeping bag close to her chest. Though she wasn't cold, hugging the soft material comforted her. "I have a plan."

"Of that, the Sovereign has confirmed," Gabe said. "But the details have not yet been revealed to me."

"I doubt it matters. What's that thing the army says about plans?"

Gabe smiled. "No plan survives first contact with the enemy."

"Yeah, that."

"May I presume you intend to start your day at school?" Gabe tipped his head in that direction.

"Yes. I have an important letter for Chloe . . . or can I just give it to you to pass on?"

Gabe shook his head. "That wouldn't be wise." He shuddered.

Given that Gabe unsettled Chloe, Emma accepted her mentor's answer. "Okay then. Once I deliver the letter, I'll head to the Temple. I'll stay the night, and at midnight I'll approach the Sovereign to ask for the appointment of a new High Priest. And if I die trying, I believe an eternal reward awaits me."

Gabe sputtered out a chuckle. "A bit melodramatic, don't you think, my child?"

"I'm trying to be realistic." Though endearing, continually referring to her as *my child* was becoming wearisome. He talked highly of her but kept implying she was a kid.

"Why not be optimistic instead?" Gabe said. "You're supported by the Holy Text, many intercede on your behalf, and the Sovereign waits to receive you."

"Has the Sovereign told you that?"

"I have faith."

"I wish I had a tad more," Emma said with a hopeful sigh.

Gabe ignored her words. "We have time before your mission commences. I presume you have more questions?"

Emma did, but a different one escaped her mouth. "Do your son and granddaughter live in the city? Is that why you're here?"

"Yes, they reside nearby. I observe my granddaughter from a distance." Gabe dropped his head into his hands. "She has no aura and only the faintest of color."

"What's her name?" Emma perked up. "Maybe I know her."

Gabe shook his head. "I've already said too much. What is your other question? The real one."

"Can you teach me to see if people have the Sovereign's light within them?"

"I can point you in the proper direction, but the outcome resides within."

Why are his answers always so cryptic? "We've got two hours," Emma said. "I'm listening."

"Remember how I guided you yesterday to internalize the passage you wanted to memorize? To open your essence to receive? To meditate? To seek the supernatural Divine?"

"I remember. But I don't understand."

"To see in the spiritual realm, you must close your eyes to the physical. To hear the supernatural, you must stop listening to the corporeal."

"That's as clear as mud."

"Patience, young one. This takes years for people to master—if at all—yet you expect to do it in two hours."

"People call me an overachiever." Emma's eyes twinkled at Gabe.

"Very well. Close your eyes. Tune out every-thing but the sound of my voice. Picture me in your soul. Open yourself to perceive my essence."

Emma breathed in. She breathed out. Like yesterday, she did as Gabe instructed.

She opened her spirit to receive supernatural insight. At last, Gabe's image materialized in her mind. A light emanated from his body. It came, faint at first, as if looking into a dim mirror. Then clarity emerged. The light grew brighter, not a pure white glow but a soothing yellow hue. Emma saw the Sovereign's Divine Spirit living inside of Gabe.

"Yellow," she mumbled.

"You are an astute student, young one."

"And you are an excellent teacher, old man."

I don't know what to call you. Gabe's thoughts drifted into Emma's head. *You don't appreciate "my child" and you don't like "young one" either.*

Why not call me Emma? she thought.

Emma it is. From this point forward and forevermore, so it shall be, came back Gabe's thoughts.

"Wait!" Emma said. Her eyes burst open as she gawked at Gabe. "Were we just communicating in the supernatural realm? Like telepathy or some-thing? I thought that was a myth."

"Myths are often how the uninitiated explain

away spiritual truth," Gabe said. "It's not telepathy, per se. It exists as something substantially different and profoundly better."

Emma's shoulders sagged. "I have so much to learn."

"A young girl approaches. Hone your newfound skill on her."

"Emma?" Sarah's voice wafted up from below. "I have breakfast. Lower the rope."

Soon Emma had hauled up her next meal. Seconds later, Sarah's head poked through the opening in the platform. Doing a double take, the young girl stared at the man sitting cross-legged on the floor. Her shocked eyes flickered with recognition. "Are you Gabe? You look just like the guy in my dream. Joshua said your name is Gabe."

"I am he." The old man dipped his head in confirmation.

"Wait a minute!" Emma shrieked. "You know Joshua?"

"Gabe told Joshua to read the Holy Text each morning," Sarah said. "I've been reading it too. It's really rad."

"Rad?" Emma scrunched her eyebrows.

"You know, radical."

As Emma processed this news, she unpacked

the bountiful breakfast Sarah's mom had prepared: scrambled eggs, toast, bacon, cantaloupe, and apple juice. Dividing the ample meal in half, she offered one part to Gabe. She expected him to decline, assuming he didn't need to eat, but he accepted it with no hesitation. He chomped into the toast, chewing with open-mouth enthusiasm and spewing crumbs everywhere.

I guess he's just a man after all and not some angel thingy, Emma thought.

I heard that. Gabe smirked in his spirit.

This mind-reading bit is already getting old, Emma responded through her thoughts.

Blocking others from access is possible, Gabe countered mentally, *but it requires much practice.*

Then I'll begin right away, came Emma's quick reply. *Starting now!*

Gabe turned to Sarah. "You have a question you want to ask of me. Is that correct, my girl?

Her name is Sarah, interjected Emma through her thoughts.

I heard that, Gabe responded nonverbally. *Prohibiting my access to your mind will take time.*

I wasn't trying to block you, Emma thought. *I wanted you to hear.* She tried to bar further access to her mind, even though she wasn't quite sure she was even doing it—or if she could do it again.

"I'm confused about this body, soul, and spirit thing," Sarah said, answering Gabe's earlier question.

"A wise request for elucidation," the old man replied. "Your body—our physical reality—is most tangible and most temporary. Our spirits exist in the supernatural realm. The spirit is unseen to most from this vantage, yet it will live on into eternity. Our souls connect the two."

"What's a soul?" Sarah asked.

Yes, I want to know too, Emma thought, making sure not to block this from Gabe.

"Ah, yes," Gabe said. "The soul is key. Your soul is that which is known but unseen. It comprises what you think, what you want, and how you feel."

Sarah was quiet for a moment. Then her face brightened. "You mean our mind, will, and emotions?"

"Yes indeed. Well said, my dear Sarah," Gabe confirmed.

"Hey! You know my name? How?"

"Emma told me."

"When?" Sarah's gaze jumped from Gabe to Emma. "I didn't hear her say a thing."

"We communicate on a different plane, one that you presently lack access to but one day soon will. If you desire to pursue it, I can guide you, just as I have for Joshua and for Emma. But not today. A later time is warranted."

Though Emma's ears took in this exchange in the temporal realm, her eyes sought Sarah in the spiritual. The girl's image appeared, just as Gabe's had earlier. In her spirit, Emma watched as a soft light materialized from Sarah's essence. The light shone brighter and settled on a soft ruby red. The meaning was clear. The Sovereign's presence also lived in Sarah. Emma couldn't wait to try her newfound skill on her family, on Chloe, and especially on Joshua.

"Oh no!" Sarah exclaimed. "Going to be late. Gotta bounce." The girl scrambled down the ladder.

Without a word, Gabe left too.

14

PLANS CHANGE

Emma studied the school building from the safety of the tree house. The teachers arrived, and the students came. But she saw no police cars or SWAT vehicles. She waited until second period started before she climbed down.

A new plan emerged. She'd slip into school through the back doors, slide the letters into Chloe's locker, and retreat. *Easy-peasy*. Then, she'd head to the Temple. New moon or not, she'd wait in the Temple sanctuary. At midnight she'd implore the Sovereign to provide a new High Priest. If she failed, she'd likely die, but if she succeeded, the new High Priest would fix everything.

Midway through second period, Emma eased

into the school building unobserved. The halls were empty. The security cameras watched her movements, but she ducked her head and figured she'd surely be gone before anyone knew she was there. She slipped the notes into Chloe's locker and retraced her steps.

She hadn't made it far when the school's PA system clicked on. "Emma Barlow, you're not as smart as you think." The voice sounded like Hernandez, the menacing SWAT captain from the other day. "We have your little friend. If you exit via the front doors and surrender, we'll let her go. Otherwise, we'll arrest her in your place."

Sovereign, save Chloe and protect me! Don't let my mission end before it begins. Deliver me from this corrupt man. May it be so.

A calm assurance overcame Emma. Bold confidence surged through her. Somehow—though she didn't know how—this was all going to work out. An overwhelming peace filled her. Emma turned and strode toward the front doors as commanded. She even smiled at the security cameras and waved.

She walked out of the school building to face a dozen officers. They stood with smug satisfaction in the parking lot, ready to arrest her. Behind them stood Hernandez, a pleased smirk painted on his face as he clutched a trembling Chloe.

"Let her go," Emma said, "and I'll come to you." Several officers raised their military rifles in case she failed to follow through.

Hernandez released Chloe, and she walked toward Emma. Only then did Emma move forward. As they passed each other, Emma whispered, "It's okay. Check your locker."

Chloe ran into the school building as Emma continued her confident march toward the soldiers. Without a fight, she let them arrest her and handcuff her to two officers. Hernandez guided them all into an armored police van that had just pulled up.

"You'll love our retraining program," Hernandez said with a sneer before he slammed the back doors of the van shut.

Handcuffed to a guard on each side, Emma fell into one of them as the van lurched forward.

Sovereign, I know you have this all worked out. Show me what to do when the time comes.

A few minutes later, the van pulled to a stop, no doubt at a traffic light. Both guards had their eyes closed and their heads tipped back. *Lift your arms,* came the Sovereign's words inside her head.

Emma obeyed. To her astonishment, both

handcuffs opened with a click and fell off. Her heart pounded. *What's happening?* Emma asked the Sovereign.

Leave, came the Divine's response.

Watching the two men, Emma crept to the back of the van, opened a door, and slid out. She eased the door shut, but it latched with a loudness she was sure would wake the guards. But she heard no movement inside. She reached the sidewalk just as the light turned green and the van took off.

Astonished, Emma watched it pull away.

What are you doing? came the Sovereign's words. *Waiting for them to return? Move!*

Emma ducked into an alley and ran two full blocks before stopping. The Sovereign's words flowed into her thoughts, pushing aside her own. Following the Sovereign's instructions—*right, left,* and *straight; faster, slower,* and *pause*—she worked her way toward the Temple, navigating alleys and side roads as she moved away from the city and into suburbia. Doing everything the Sovereign said, she walked through backyards, scrambled over a few fences, and even waded a stream.

It took hours, but she eventually reached the Temple grounds. Emma paused at its grandeur.

Though she'd come here many times by car, this

was her first time on foot. The steep incline of the drive surprised her. This might be the most physically challenging part of her journey. She breathed out a prayer of thanksgiving for protection so far, followed by a request for energy to make it up the long hill. She sucked in a deep breath and began her climb.

Straight ahead sat the ancient Temple. To its right, the new worship auditorium dwarfed it. Next to the auditorium, on the highest elevation of the entire campus, towered the impressive Temple Palace, where the High Priest lived. Its opulence, however, failed to impress Emma. *I'm so glad I don't live there.*

Midway on her approach, she paused her ascent, panting for desperate breaths. Her knees ached and her thighs throbbed in protest to her exertion. *If only the Sovereign could whisk me to the top.* It had happened to a prophet of old, why not again today? But she dared not make such a bold request.

Emma resumed her arduous path upward. Her eyes panned to the left of the ancient Temple. Next to it stood the former auditorium, along with the shuttered Temple school. At one time, the plan was to raze both to erect a 10,000-seat auditorium to replace the current one. But lacking the funds to do so, both sat unused. It didn't much matter, however, because Sunday attendance was dropping, not increasing, with only two or three hundred people showing up most weeks.

Emma's body shook for the last hundred or so steps as her lungs burned and her thighs screamed in pain. Finally, she reached the Temple.

Walking inside, she felt safe at last. Her destiny awaited. Whatever happened tonight would determine her future, along with everyone else's.

15

THE TEMPLE

L arge, quarried stones comprised most of the Temple. Massive wooden beams supported the roof of the ancient structure, with strategically placed columns throughout. There was but one double-door entrance. All the windows were boarded shut.

The only changes in the past century were the addition of a few lights, connected to electrical cords that brought in the needed power from outside, and a modern lock added to keep out nighttime treasure hunters and riffraff.

Among the many pilgrims, a handful of tourists, and a few brown-robed priests, Emma's presence in the Temple went unquestioned. Either they hadn't seen her on the news, or it was too dim for them to recognize her.

Or perhaps the Sovereign is hiding my presence from them.

Emma moved toward the altar at the far end of the Temple. The altar's substantial girth seemed to warn her to keep a safe distance. With cautious intention, she inched forward and slid into the front row. The rigid, wooden bench lacked any hint of comfort. She squirmed to conform to its unforgiving frame. Within seconds, her back ached.

Emma bowed her head, not in prayer but in reverent silence before the Almighty. Now was not a time for prayerful petition but for penitent posture. "Approach the Sovereign with a pure heart and live; those with selfish intent will perish," she quoted from the Holy Text in a barely audible whisper. It was the passage Gabe had shown her the day before and which she had already memorized.

If only she could better understand how to put this mysterious instruction into practice. She opened her mind to receive illumination from the Sovereign, but no words of clarity came, only silence in the supernatural realm. *Is this all a huge mistake?* she wondered. *Am I about to die?*

Yet peace filled Emma's soul at that thought. She was, in fact, where she needed to be, and at the ideal time. She was sure. Only the outcome remained in doubt. In a few hours, she would know.

At sunset, the priests prepared to lock up for the night.

"We're closing up, miss," one priest said. "You need to leave."

"I'm staying." Emma turned and scowled at the middle-aged man. "At midnight, I'm going to ask the Sovereign to send us a new High Priest."

"You will surely perish, just like all the others who have preceded you. Or you'll go completely mad."

"I'm not like all the others."

"You're just a girl."

"I'm going to try." Emma narrowed her gaze at the insulting man. "Which is more than I can say for you."

"As you wish." The man gave the slightest downward tip of his head and backed away.

"I am a child of the Sovereign. This is where I belong."

A few other priests approached. They circled her and extended their palms toward her. "May the

Sovereign bless you," they intoned in unison. "May the Sovereign protect you. May the Sovereign hear your plea."

"And may the Sovereign spare your life," the first priest mumbled as the others walked away. Once everyone else left, he unplugged the lights and locked the Temple doors behind him.

The darkness filled Emma with peace. She was in the right place, at the right time. *Sovereign, I don't know what I'm supposed to say or do. Please receive my efforts as an offering to you, an act of worship from the depths of my heart. Amen.*

Emma sat and began reciting some of the Holy Text she had memorized. She also sang songs of worship to the Sovereign, ones she remembered from the Sunday services. She remained sitting in the soothing darkness, alternating between prayer, Scripture, and song.

All concerns vanished. Life no longer mattered. Emma's spirit connected with the Almighty on a higher plane. Though she'd encountered brief glimpses of this in the past, her experience here at the Temple was both prolonged and intense.

"I know you are here, Sovereign." Emma stood. Midnight or not, she wasn't sure, but now was her moment. She lifted her hands. "I sense your presence and am honored by it. Will you provide us with a new High Priest to guide us and release our people from prison? Show me what to do, and I'll do it."

Though locked inside a closed building, a gentle breeze caressed Emma's cheek. Cool. Refreshing. As the breeze continued to blow, its intensity grew into a rushing wind. Emma quivered. Her body shook with uncontrollable tremors. Fear gripped her heart and squeezed hard. Surely the strengthening force meant to kill her. If this was the end of her life, she was ready to accept the Sovereign's will.

Emma dropped and prostrated herself. Her muscles tensed and then locked. She could no longer move. A warmth enveloped her, at first a soothing contrast to the Temple's cold, marble floor, but then it grew hotter. Beads of sweat formed on her face. Unable to move, she couldn't wipe them away. They dripped to the floor.

Though once inseparable, her intertwined body and spirit now eased apart. It was a peaceful separation and not an abrupt jerk. Emma's essence left her shell. Was she dead?

Her incorporeal self stirred and levitated as her body remained immobile. *At least I'm going up.* Her physical form on the Temple floor no longer seemed real. It was her, and yet it wasn't. Though she now had no body, her spirit experienced the sensation of her arms and legs falling limp. And she sensed hair blowing back from her face.

Emma's spirit continued rising, and soon she could no longer make out her body below. It didn't matter anyway. A warm peace filled her. Yet she wondered about her family and friends. Were her parents okay? The twins? What about Chloe and . . .?

She pushed the thought of Joshua away from her mind before it could fully form. If she still had a head, she would have shaken it with vigor. With her life as she knew it over, and the afterlife before her, this was no time to dwell on Joshua.

Her disembodied self slid into an ethereal realm. It was a safe place, safer than she could have ever imagined. It was soothing, airy, bright. Oh, so bright. If she had hands, she would've shielded herself from the near-blinding blaze of this immaterial place.

An even brighter orb drifted toward her. It was the Sovereign. Emma knew for sure.

"The next High Priest must have a pure heart," the Sovereign said in response to the question

Emma had spoken seconds earlier, but which seemed a lifetime away.

Emma's spirit soared at the ethereal sound. So clear, so gentle, yet firm. Of the world, yet not of the world. "If I can help from this distant place, show me how to find such a person."

"The next High Priest must also share my perspective," the Sovereign said.

"What would you have me do now that I'm dead?"

"You have a pure heart. You're beginning to grasp my perspective. I choose you as the new High Priest," declared the Sovereign.

Emma's thoughts spun at this revelation. "No way! The High Priest must be someone older, educated, and experienced."

"But that's not who I want. I want you."

Emma thought about saying no, but she sensed the Sovereign was right—even if the thought of being the new High Priest shocked her. In truth, it terrified her. "Even if you raise me from the dead, I'm not ready."

"For months you've been studying the Holy Text every night. I say you are as ready as you will ever be. Move forward in faith and trust me with the rest."

"But I'm dead."

"Your time has not yet come. You are but a visitor here and not a resident."

"You mean . . . I can go back?"

"Yes," the Sovereign said. "You can . . . and you will."

Emma gasped. "When?"

"*When* does not exist in this place. Yesterday, today, and tomorrow are all one. You now exist outside the time-space reality I created."

"What about my parents? Hailey and Brayden? And Chloe?"

"Although quite worried about you, your parents are fine. Your siblings are sleeping soundly in their beds. Chloe is okay too—quite fine, really. And I am with Joshua in jail."

"I didn't ask about him!" Emma sputtered.

"But you were thinking about him."

"He's just an irritating guy who won't leave me alone."

"But you do think about him. In fact, you've even thought about kissing him."

"Now *you're* starting to irritate me!" Emma gasped and wished she still had a hand to put over her nonexistent mouth that kept saying things it shouldn't.

The Sovereign laughed.

This shocked Emma. She had envisioned the Sovereign as someone to fear, yet the Almighty was emerging as something quite likable. As some*one* quite likable.

"Joshua will be all right, and you will have your chance to kiss him. Soon."

This promise both thrilled and terrified Emma. The boy irked her to no end, yet something about him was also quite attractive. She changed the subject. "How in the world am I supposed to be the High Priest? I'm just a kid—a girl. I'm not ready!"

"First," the Sovereign said, "you *will* be the next High Priest. And second, no one is ever ready for such a role. I will provide what you need, when you need it. All I require from you is that you trust me and obey, just as when I guided you home the other night and after you escaped from the SWAT van today."

"I will do as you say," Emma said with a reverent bow of her spirit. "May your will be done."

Emma's essence pulled away from the Sovereign's bright light. She tried to reach out her nonexistent arms for the Sovereign and pull the deity close. But it didn't work. Her incorporeal essence eased out of heaven. The parting, though gentle, filled her soul with a sad sense of loss. As her spirit drifted downward to her body, the glow of heaven faded, and the darkness of Earth reappeared.

Her spirit moved toward the reunion with her physical shell, gaining speed as though falling. The rapid descent toward Earth would have alarmed her in life, but, still existing only in spirit, the journey filled her with exhilaration—and awe. As her essence approached her human frame, her spirit jerked to a stop, and, with a slight thump, the two parts of her merged back into one.

Once again having a body to move, Emma righted herself from her prostrate position, wiped the beads of sweat from her face, and shook her arms with delight. Joy filled her soul, her chest bursting with glee at the reuniting of her spirit and body.

A fire ignited and hovered over the altar. The orange and yellow tongue danced in rhythmic time to an ethereal song. The single flame moved toward Emma. It came to rest on her head and melded into her body. Her face warmed, and the surrounding space glowed.

Thank you, Sovereign. I put my trust in you and will

obey what you tell me to do. Take away my doubt and fear.
Replace them with an unshakable faith in you.

As the new day approached, Emma suspected she was at last beginning to understand the Sovereign's perspective.

And that she might, in fact, be the new High Priest. But did she dare to embrace it?

16

A NEW DAY

A key slid into the lock of the Temple entrance. The tumblers released, and the doors creaked open. Light streamed into the darkness. A gush of fresh air bathed Emma's sweaty body and pushed away the musty air that had enveloped her.

Following the morning brightness came two priests. Moments later several other priests trailed behind them. The first priest dragged in an extension cord. He plugged in a light and cast its beam into the Temple. As one, the group gasped. They all bowed their heads and kneeled before her.

Emma mentally recoiled at their reaction, her body frozen for a time at their shocking display of reverence. These were adults, two or three times her age, paying her—a mere teenager—homage. She willed her eyes to not glance away, which would reveal the discomfort that filled her soul. She sucked in a slow breath, strengthening her resolve as her lungs filled with air and her soul expanded with courage.

"There is no need for this," Emma said. "I'm a person—just like you. Please stand."

"Yes, My Lord," the priests intoned in unison. They rose but continued to look down.

"Only the Sovereign is Lord. Please call me Emma."

One priest glanced up at her, but only for a moment. "Nevertheless, by tradition we always address the High Priest as 'My Lord.' It is an acknowledgment of honor."

"That honor belongs to the Sovereign alone." Emma responded with a confidence that didn't come from within. "It's time we break that tradition—starting now."

"As you wish," said the priest who seemed to take the lead. "But we request your patience as we strive to break this lifetime practice."

Emma nodded, but no one saw her confirmation. "Come, we have much to do." The bold words emanating from her mouth shocked her.

"First, you better look outside, My Lord . . . I mean, Emma," the lead priest said, while still staring at the floor.

"Oh?" Emma raised her left eyebrow. Yet no one was looking at her to notice. And no one reacted to the hitch in her voice.

"Many kept vigil throughout the night." Still looking at his feet, the priest shifted. At last, he glanced up for but a second. "Their numbers grow."

"How many?"

"Initially hundreds, now thousands. Your friend arrived first."

"Chloe!"

"Her faith is strong," another priest added. "Many more joined her, all at her urging. Even a homeless zealot."

Must be Gabe. Emma beamed with delight.

"Your family arrived early this morning."

Emma walked out of the Temple with the priests in tow. An amazed crowd of people stood arrayed in a semicircle around the entrance to the Temple. Some kept a close watch. Others bowed in humble prayer. A few gazed up to the heavens with hands raised. Behind them, a mass pressed in.

A gasp reverberated through those gathered when they saw Emma standing before them. They, too, kneeled before her, but this time their tribute didn't surprise her.

She extended her arms toward the throng and gestured for them to stand. No one did.

"See how her face glows," said one.

"Finally, someone who encountered the Sovereign and lived," said another.

"At last, we have a High Priest again. Our first High Priestess," said a third.

"All praise to the High Priestess! All praise to the High Priestess!" they chanted over and over.

Emma lifted her arms, signaling them to stop. "All praise belongs to the Sovereign." She projected her voice so the crowd could hear. "I am but a humble servant."

The people murmured their approval. Some smiled, and others ventured a cautious wave. Tears flowed down the cheeks of many.

Yet not everyone was pleased. The SWAT team was there too. As a group, they had pushed their way forward, standing but a hundred feet away. They seemed poised to arrest her.

"Surrender peacefully, and no one will get

hurt," said Captain Hernandez on his bullhorn. His officers readied their weapons, shoulders thrust back and heads held high.

The people protested at his words and pressed forward, ready to protect her, but Emma gestured for them to stand down. They did, pulling back to open the space between her and Hernandez.

"You have no authority here and no reason to arrest me," Emma said with a confidence that felt foreign.

"Seize her!" Hernandez bellowed. His charges moved forward.

Before Emma could pray for divine guidance, the answer came. *Stretch out your hands to halt their advance.*

She did. They stopped.

Most stood still. A few officers attempted to claw their way forward, but they could not, as if held back by an invisible force.

"You must leave," Emma said with a dismissive wave of her hand. Perplexed, the soldiers retreated to their vehicles and sped away, leaving only Hernandez behind with his bullhorn in one hand and a formidable assault rifle in the other.

"You can come with me peacefully," he said

through his bullhorn, "or you can leave in a box." He shifted his weapon to a more ready position. "But either way, this ends now."

"This isn't the end," Emma called out. "This is the beginning."

"Last chance." He raised his gun.

Emma didn't flinch. She was ready to die.

Hernandez dropped his bullhorn, and it crashed to the ground. He leveled his semiautomatic assault weapon at her. He fired. The crowd screamed in horror, and Emma braced herself for the pain of hot metal ripping through her flesh. But she felt nothing. Instead, the bullets stopped inches before they reached her and fell to the ground in a harmless heap.

Hernandez glared at his gun and scowled. His face reddened, and his brow tightened.

Realizing she would not die today, and emboldened by the Sovereign's protection, Emma walked toward the captain.

He resumed firing at her, his teeth gritted. But like before, the bullets fell to the ground with harmless indifference.

Emma reached him and pushed the hot barrel of his weapon aside, pointing it toward the ground.

The officer dropped his gun as if it were too blistering to hold. His face blanched and his body shook. He kneeled. "Spare me," he pleaded. "Please, don't kill me for my many failings."

"Only the Sovereign has the power and authority to take a life," Emma said. "But I do want you to return to the prison and release everyone who's there for retraining, especially Joshua Hart. Take care of this right away, and then see that everyone wrongly imprisoned across the country gets released too. Do this, and you'll receive my blessing."

"Yes, High Priestess," he said with a humble tip of his head. "I will do as you say." Still trembling, he wiped beads of sweat from his forehead and scurried away, leaving his weapon and bullhorn lying on the ground.

More people had arrived—along with the media—to witness these events. Cameras clicked, and video feeds broadcast the news throughout the nation, perhaps even around the world.

"All praise to our Sovereign Lord," Emma shouted as she raised her fist in the air.

"All praise to our Sovereign Lord," the people repeated, chanting their adoration to the Almighty over and over.

Maybe this High Priest thing will work out after all.

If you liked *Seeking the Sovereign*, please leave a review online. Your review will help others discover this book and encourage them to read it too.

Thank you.

CONFRONTING THE CHAOS
BOOK 2 OF THE NEXT HIGH PRIEST SERIES

Chapter 1: Alive

Emma shifted under the weight of warm covers. Yet something was wrong. This wasn't her bed. It didn't feel like her room. A surge of panic coursed through her body. *Where am I? What has happened?* She urged her eyes to open—and failed.

Why can't I focus? Groggy best described her mind. *Why is it so hard to move?* Or maybe achy better defined how she felt. Which was it? A confused mind or a sore body? It was too much to sort out. She couldn't concentrate. For now, she'd settle on groggy *and* achy. Her fleeting reality slipped away. Slumber overtook her.

Emma didn't know if it was seconds, minutes, or hours later when her eyes fluttered open for a moment and then flitted shut. *Where am I?* She yawned and stretched with a groan. *Why does my entire body throb?*

"I think she's finally waking up," a voice said. It sounded familiar.

"Mom?" Emma croaked. She reached out a hand to touch the voice, but, encountering nothing, her weak arm dropped helplessly to the bed. Emma sighed. Someone stroked her hand. Warm. Comforting. Safe.

"I'm right here, dear," her mom said. "We all are. Your dad and your sister and brother. Chloe and a girl named Sarah are waiting outside."

"What happened?" Emma moaned. Something was wrong. She forced her eyes open and squinted.

The image of her mom came into focus. She sat in a chair next to the bed. "You're in the High Priest's residence in the Temple Palace. I'll explain everything later, but first we need to make sure you're all right."

"I'm fine. My mind's a bit foggy. I'm sore too. I don't think that's going away anytime soon." With care, Emma shifted in the oversized bed, one far larger than she'd ever slept in—or even seen.

A jolt of pain shot from her right calf to her left shoulder, traveling through her back. She yelped as if shocked by a surge of electricity. "Ouch!" As the pain ebbed, she let out a controlled breath.

"Where does it hurt?" Her dad rose from his chair.

Emma shifted her gaze to him. "All over."

"Describe it."

She moved her arm with care and gave an unconcerned wave with the back of her hand. She wasn't being disrespectful because she knew in her spirit she was okay—at least she *would* be. She merely needed to give it time.

Her dad opened his mouth as if to protest but then closed it, saying nothing.

"When did you last eat, Emma?" Concern coated her mom's question.

With effort, Emma shifted her attention—foggy as it was—back to her mom. "I ate breakfast this morning at Sarah's."

"You mean Thursday?" Her mom sounded confused. "Before school?"

"Yes, that's what I said. This morning."

"Emma," her mom said gently, "today is Saturday. It's after noon. You've been sleeping for over twenty-four hours."

"I guess that's why I'm so hungry. And why I so need to pee." Emma let go of her mom's hand and, with effort, eased off the blankets. Taking her time, she slid her legs to the side of the bed and willed her body upright. At least she tried to. Her head spun, and she fell back onto the bed with a grunt. She stared helplessly at the ceiling.

"Do you want us to help you?"

Emma forced her eyes to take in the whole room to see who *us* referred to. Her mom stretched out a hand. Her dad stood next to her mom. The twins kept vigil at the foot of the bed, concern painted on their uncharacteristically cherub faces. With a deliberate slowness, Emma sat up again and extended both arms. Her mom took one and her dad held the other. Leaning on them for support, she stood, but she didn't know which direction to head. "Ah, where's the bathroom?"

Her sister giggled. "We've found at least six so far. The closest one is over there." Hailey pointed to Emma's right. Her parents guided her in that direction.

When finished, she caught her reflection in the bathroom mirror. She paused in distress at what looked back at her. Having not been washed in three days, her hair showed it, no longer clean and fluffy—instead, oily and matted.

She pushed the tangled, hazel mess away from her face, which revealed a smear of dirt across her left cheek and a zit about ready to erupt on her forehead. Lacking her compact or any other helpful resources, all she could do was scrape her fingernail over it to release the pressure. It worked. Sort of. *Gross. Oh, so gross.*

She corralled her hair and—lacking a hair clip or ponytail holder—she looped it over itself in a loose knot. It would have to do for now.

She shuffled back to the bed on her own and fell into it with a moan. "Maybe after I get something to eat, I'll be strong enough to take a shower. I feel gross." She ran her tongue over her teeth. *Definitely gross.*

Her dad tipped his head toward her brother, who scurried from the room. Emma hoped he was going to round up some food.

"What's the last thing you remember?" Dad asked.

Emma's mind clawed through a jumbled heap of memories. One image emerged and became clearer. "I spent the night in the Temple and talked with the Sovereign about giving us a new High Priest."

Her parents shared concerned glances.

"I never wanted it to be me."

Her mom raised an eyebrow toward Emma's dad.

Emma clawed her mind for clarity. Some images emerged, faint at first and then clearer. "In the morning, there was a confrontation outside with the SWAT team. The captain was mad and . . . he shot at me with his machine gun." Emma gasped at the thought. "But the bullets fell to the ground before they hit me." She glanced at her chest to make sure she was okay. "The Sovereign protected me."

Emma's mind struggled to recall what happened next. "I sent the captain back to the prison to release Joshua—to free all the prisoners wrongly arrested."

Emma shut her eyes as she struggled to pull the next events from her mind. "There were a lot of people there . . . and the media with their cameras and mics. I don't know if I said something to the crowd or just thought about it . . . The next thing I remember is waking up here."

"You did, indeed, speak to the crowd," her dad

said. "The media captured everything and broadcast it across the country—around the world. You're a hero, by the way. We couldn't be prouder.

"The grand celebration lasted for hours," he added. "More and more people kept arriving. Thousands, for sure. I suspect even ten. You thanked them for coming and showing their support. Then you excused yourself to get some needed rest. You went back into the Temple and collapsed just inside."

That last part was a blur. Emma couldn't decide if she remembered that happening or merely wanted to.

"What you went through is unprecedented," her dad said. "The medical community has no explanation for what your body—and your mind—endured throughout all that happened to you. Both the night spent in the Temple—which has killed everyone else or drove them to madness—and your body repelling bullets."

"The Sovereign protected me." This was all the explanation Emma could offer—and all that she needed. "I'm sore, and it's hard to focus, but I'm okay. Or at least I will be."

"Though you underwent an extraordinary trauma, I can confirm your body hasn't suffered as a result. Your temperature is normal, your pulse is steady, and your heart is strong. As a doctor, I prescribe rest. As your father, I'm nonetheless concerned."

"I'm fine. No worries."

But am I?

Continue reading *Confronting the Chaos*, Book 2 of The Next High Priest Series.

ABOUT PETER DEHAAN

Peter DeHaan is an adult who dreams of being a teenager. When he's not contemplating grown-up thoughts, his mind retreats to the domain of invented worlds with his loyal and most real, yet still imaginary, friends. What grand adventures they have: righting wrongs, solving problems, and making their world a better place to live.

His first published adventures come to life in "The Next High Priest Series"—a faith-friendly speculative fiction adventure in a world just like ours . . . only different.

Next up is *The Curious Gift*, a YA contemporary novella with a hint of the supernatural.

Then comes "The Ice Creamed Series," a present-day quest for friendship and love, all the while trying to survive high school unscathed and ping-ponging between responsible impulses and irresponsible slipups.

Want more? Get a free short-story prequel about Emma along with updates of upcoming books when you sign up for Peter's fiction newsletter at PeterDeHaan.com/fiction.

9 7 9 8 8 8 8 0 9 0 9 8 5